Dear Parent:
Your child's love of reading starts here!

Every child learns to read in a different way and at his or her own speed. Some go back and forth between reading levels and read favorite books again and again. Others read through each level in order. You can help your young reader improve and become more confident by encouraging his or her own interests and abilities. From books your child reads with you to the first books he or she reads alone, there are I Can Read Books for every stage of reading:

SHARED READING
Basic language, word repetition, and whimsical illustrations, ideal for sharing with your emergent reader

BEGINNING READING
Short sentences, familiar words, and simple concepts for children eager to read on their own

READING WITH HELP
Engaging stories, longer sentences, and language play for developing readers

READING ALONE
Complex plots, challenging vocabulary, and high-interest topics for the independent reader

ADVANCED READING
Short paragraphs, chapters, and exciting themes for the perfect bridge to chapter books

I Can Read Books have introduced children to the joy of reading since 1957. Featuring award-winning authors and illustrators and a fabulous cast of beloved characters, I Can Read Books set the standard for beginning readers.

A lifetime of discovery begins with the magical words **"I Can Read!"**

*Visit www.icanread.com for information
on enriching your child's reading experience.*

Pinkalicious®
Fairy House

For Sydney!
xox,
Aunt Victoria

The author gratefully acknowledges
the artistic and editorial contributions
of Daniel Griffo and Natalie Engel.

I Can Read Book® is a trademark of HarperCollins Publishers.

Pinkalicious: Fairy House
Copyright © 2013 by Victoria Kann

PINKALICIOUS and all related logos and characters are trademarks of Victoria Kann. Used with permission.

Based on the HarperCollins book *Pinkalicious* written by
Victoria Kann and Elizabeth Kann, illustrated by Victoria Kann
All rights reserved. Printed in the United States of America.
No part of this book may be used or reproduced in any manner whatsoever without
written permission except in the case of brief quotations embodied in critical articles and reviews.
For information address HarperCollins Children's Books, a division of HarperCollins Publishers,
195 Broadway, New York, NY 10007.
www.icanread.com

Library of Congress catalog card number: 2012940910
ISBN 978-0-06-218783-3 (trade bdg.) — ISBN 978-0-06-218782-6 (pbk.)

16 17 18 PC/WOR 10 9 8 7 6 5 4 3
❖
First Edition

I Can Read!

BEGINNING 1 READING

Pinkalicious®
Fairy House

by Victoria Kann

HARPER

An Imprint of HarperCollinsPublishers

It was spring,
my favorite season.
I love how the sky looks like
cotton candy at sunset.

Every spring, our garden comes alive
with blossoms of every color.
I know why our garden
is so beautiful.
It's because of the fairies!

Fairies come to our yard
and sprinkle fairy dust
to make the plants grow.
I have never seen them,
but I know that they are real.
I can see sparkles outside my window.

This spring, I had a plan.

I would see the fairies!

"Pinkalicious, what are you doing?"

asked Peter as I collected

twigs and leaves.

"I'm making a house
for the fairies to live in.
Then they can live in our garden
and we will be able to see them,"
I said.

11

"I want to see them, too!

Let me help," said Peter.

He brought out his shell collection.

"Let's build the house here
in the garden," I said.
"Fairies are sure to come this way."

Piece by piece,

we built a little house.

I wove buttercups

around the door.

Peter made a pathway

with his shells.

13

Soon we had a cozy home
for the fairies.
I couldn't wait for them to come.
Every day I watched the house
from my swing.

I made a pond, a boat,

and even a slide

for the fairies to find.

But the fairies did not come.

When Peter saw how sad I looked

he said, "Cheer up—the pink flower buds

are blooming!"

But I wanted to see the fairies!

Suddenly, I had an idea.

"Maybe the fairies only come out at night," I said.

"Maybe they only sprinkle fairy dust by moonlight!"

I told Mommy and Daddy
what I wanted to do.
They let Peter and me camp out
and keep watch for the fairies.

That evening, Peter and I
spread out our sleeping bags.
I left the fairies a sweet snack
of honeysuckle and berries.

"Do you think they will come?"
asked Peter.
"Yes," I said,
and added in a whisper,
"I really, really hope so."

21

We told each other stories
until Peter fell asleep.
As the night got darker
I heard crickets and owls,
but not a single fairy.

Once I thought I heard
some soft, gentle humming.
It was just Peter.
He was snoring.

I did everything I could
to stay awake.
I looked up at the moon.
I counted the stars.
I didn't want to miss the fairies.

24

But as I counted the stars,
my eyelids got heavy.
I couldn't help it.
I drifted off to sleep.

The next thing I knew,

I heard a bird singing.

I opened my eyes.

It was dawn.

I heard hushed voices in the garden.

Mommy and Daddy

were looking at something together.

"How beautiful!" they said.

As I stretched,

a sweet smell filled the air.

All around me,

colorful flowers were in full bloom.

I looked at the fairy house.

The honeysuckle and berries

were gone.

"The fairies came!" I cried.

"They came,

but I missed the whole thing."

Peter started to sniffle.

"Don't cry. Look!" I said.

Up in the air

I could see glimmers of light

shooting across

the early-morning sky.

"Fairies." I gasped.

The light shimmered

brighter and brighter

until it sparkled into sunshine.

"I knew you were real," I said.

My family and I

watched the sun come up.

"Thank you, fairies," I whispered.

Wherever they were,

I knew they could hear me.